P9-DNF-834

ORCA
YOUNG
READERS

1145

Any Pet Will Do

Nancy Shouse

WITHDRAWN

Library Media Center
Washington School
3 Sage Drive
Monticello, IL 61856

ORCA BOOK PUBLISHERS

Copyright © 2005 Nancy Shouse

All rights reserved. No part of this publication may be reproduced or transmitted in any form or by any means, electronic or mechanical, including photocopying, recording or by any information storage and retrieval system now known or to be invented, without permission in writing from the publisher.

National Library of Canada Cataloguing in Publication Data:

Shouse, Nancy, 1956-
Any pet will do / Nancy Shouse.

(Orca young readers)
ISBN 1-55143-354-0

I. Title. II. Series.

PS8637.H68A65 2005   jC813'.6   C2005-901081-9

First Published in the United States 2005

Library of Congress Control Number: 2005922032

Summary: Jeremy pet-sits his neighbors' pets in an effort to discover which pet will best suit him.

Free teachers' guide available. www.orcabook.com

Orca Book Publishers gratefully acknowledges the support for its publishing programs provided by the following agencies: the Government of Canada through the Department of Canadian Heritage's Book Publishing Industry Development Program (BPIDP), the Canada Council for the Arts, and the British Columbia Arts Council.

Cover design and typesetting by Lynn O'Rourke
Cover & interior illustrations by Esme Nichola Shilletto

In Canada:	In the United States:
Orca Book Publishers	Orca Book Publishers
Box 5626 Stn. B	PO Box 468
Victoria, BC Canada	Custer, WA USA
V8R 6S4	98240-0468

08 07 06 05 • 6 5 4 3 2 1

Printed and bound in Canada.

For Zachary, Anna and Elliot

The Terrible Truth

Four years ago, when Jeremy Jeffers turned five, he made an awful discovery: Not one of his little collection of stuffed animals magically sprang to life at night. Instead of romping around the house, messing up the sofa cushions and making sticky jam sandwiches, Tough Ted and the rest of the gang stayed in tangled clumps on the bedroom floor—not stirring, not breathing and certainly not having any fun!

From that moment on, Jeremy set his heart on getting a real live animal.

Now Jeremy was nine and he had waited long enough. It was time to convince his parents.

The Plan Is Hatched

"Pets are a huge responsibility," Jeremy's father said, "especially for a nine-year-old." He picked Jeremy's coat up off the floor and hung it in the closet.

"I can be responsible!"

"A pet is not like a stuffed animal you grow tired of and stick up on a shelf," his mother added. "Having a pet is like having your very own child. They depend on you for everything, Jeremy—good food, lots of exercise and oodles of attention—and all without you ever being reminded."

"I can do all that!"

"Maybe...maybe you can." Jeremy's father stooped to pick up a small, stinky sock. "What sort of pet did you have in mind?"

Jeremy looked blank. After four years to mull it over, he still didn't have a clue. "Something soft and cuddly would be nice," he said finally. "We could snuggle in bed and read adventure stories together."

Mr. Jeffers winked at his wife. "How about this idea. Why don't you offer to pet-sit for the neighbors? Maybe that'll give you an idea of what suits you."

"Make some notices and pop them in the neighborhood mailboxes," his mother suggested. "Get Murphy to help you."

Murphy was Jeremy's number one best friend in the whole world. They pretty much stuck together like glue. Mr. Jeffers always joked that Jeremy without Murphy was like popcorn without butter—there was just something missing!

And the best thing about having a buddy who lived two houses away was that when Jeremy hung up the phone and started to count, Murphy usually barreled through the front door before he got up to twenty-nine.

Jeremy plunked a stack of his father's computer paper on the table and picked a bright red marker out of the pack. "Okay, Murph, tell me. How do I begin?"

"Say you're in training," Murphy said, dunking his molasses cookie in his glass of milk. "Say you're trying to get a bit of experience before you get your own pet."

Jeremy doodled on the paper. "I wonder if I'm allowed to be picky? I mean, what if someone shows up with a llama or something?"

Murphy laughed. "You ever see a llama prancing down MacPherson Street? The worst that could happen is my mom drops off her bucket of compost worms for you to feed."

"Don't give her any ideas!" Jeremy said, scrunching his nose. "That mucky old bucket is gross!"

Then, while Murphy sucked and nibbled on his soggy cookie, Jeremy sucked and nibbled on his bottom lip, waiting for an idea to strike.

Bingo!

Using his neatest, most smudge-free

printing, Jeremy huddled over a clean sheet of paper and went to work.

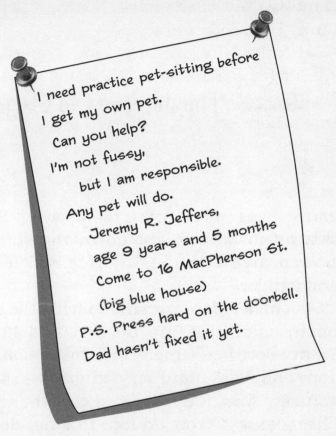

I need practice pet-sitting before
I get my own pet.
Can you help?
I'm not fussy,
    but I am responsible.
Any pet will do.
    Jeremy R. Jeffers,
    age 9 years and 5 months
Come to 16 MacPherson St.
    (big blue house)
P.S. Press hard on the doorbell.
Dad hasn't fixed it yet.

"What do you think?"

Murphy grabbed a purple marker and began to copy word for word. "I think this is going to be an interesting experiment," he said. "Very interesting!"

The Jeffers Go Gaga

Beauty was the first to arrive. She belonged to Mrs. Flight down the street, who appeared with the tiny blue budgie on her shoulder.

"Sing to her, Jeremy, sing to her!" the old woman said, mussing up Jeremy's hair. "Beauty loves a tune. Christmas songs, happy birthday, nursery rhymes—she's not fussy." Mrs. Flight peered over the tops of her glasses. "You *do* like to sing, don't you? School choir perhaps?"

Jeremy gulped. He didn't want to confess that he quit the choir because it cut into his playtime, so he quickly changed the topic.

"Why don't you keep it in there?" he asked, pointing to the large birdcage on the steps.

"Why, Jeremy, it should be perfectly obvious," Mrs. Flight said, jiggling the cage. "Do you see one spare inch of room?"

She had a point. The cage was jammed with teeny mirrors, pebbly perches, brass bells, dangling shapes and pecking toys in every color of the rainbow.

Mrs. Flight blushed. "I can't help myself," she confessed. "I go into a store with the best intentions of staying clear of the pet department, but then…well…before you know it I'm out the door with another precious little trinket." She and the budgie nuzzled nose-to-beak. "My Beauty simply loves to be surrounded by beautiful birdie things!"

The old woman's tone then became serious. "Now, watch closely," she said. "It's time for you to take over."

She held out a finger and Beauty hopped on, twittering happily. Slowly, Mrs. Flight moved her finger next to Jeremy's shoulder. "Transfer, Lovey, transfer!" she crooned.

But instead of hopping across to Jeremy, the bird's toes gripped her finger like glue.

"Hmm. Very strange," Mrs. Flight muttered. "Perhaps she senses some jitteriness in your shoulder area. Try relaxing, Jeremy. Come on, deep breaths. Follow me now—breathe in, breathe out, relax." She massaged his right shoulder with a thick, meaty thumb. "That's it," she said. "I feel the tension slipping away, melting like butter!"

Beauty apparently agreed for she made a dainty hop-skip-jump and landed squarely on the shoulder seam of Jeremy's T-shirt.

Mrs. Flight was ecstatic. "There now, that wasn't so bad, was it, Munchkin? You probably thought the boy was a nasty old cat getting ready to pounce."

Whew! With the bird finally on his shoulder, Jeremy started to feel more confident. Being mistaken for a cat would be no way to begin his first pet-sitting job!

"You know," Mrs. Flight cautioned, "Beauty may be a trifle shy starting off, what with a new house and three strangers and all. Don't be alarmed if she retreats to her perch for the entire weekend, cramped living conditions or not. Oh well, doesn't matter..." She leaned over for one last nose-to-beak kiss goodbye. "You can still admire her through the bars!"

"Uh, Mrs. Flight..."

"Yes, my sweet dumpling...oops, I mean Jeremy."

"Does the bird like listening to Minky Moore adventure stories?"

"My dear boy! Minky, Dinky, Pinky— it doesn't matter! My Beauty is positively hypnotized by the human voice."

Mr. Jeffers was about to take his first scalding sip of morning coffee when he felt a fluttering sensation near his left ear. He gave his lobe a little rub and went back to his crossword puzzle. Thinking of a three-letter word for *wise as an*__ __ __ had him so baffled that he didn't notice Jeremy breeze into the kitchen swinging a big wire cage.

"You'll never believe it!" Jeremy said. "A pet finally showed up at the door!"

His mother took a cereal bowl from the cupboard. "Let me guess," she said. "You're bird-sitting?"

Jeremy's toothy grin stretched clear across his face. "Yup," he said proudly. "A tiny blue budgie. Her name's Beauty."

Budgie! That got his father's ears buzzing! "A bird you say? Delightful! I've always had a hankering for feathers." He squinted at the empty cage. "Where is it?"

"On your head, Dad. I think it likes you."

Mr. Jeffers raced to the mirror in the hall. "Well, I'll be…" He turned his head from side to side, admiring the delicate wavy lines and broad twisty neck. "I like to fancy myself a bird person," he said. "There's something about the chirp. It actually gives me tingles."

Beauty seemed to enjoy bouncing back to the table on a cushion of hair.

"Dad, can I throw some Cheerios on your head for Beauty to peck?"

"Why not start pecking at your own cereal before it gets soggy," his mother said. "You have to leave for school in— "

"Don't say anything! Not one word!" Mr. Jeffers waggled his hands in the air like a lunatic. "What's a five-letter word for *hopping mad*?"

Jeremy and his mother looked at each other, lips zipped shut.

"Did you hear that?"

"Hear what?" asked Jeremy. "You told us not to speak."

"*Livid*—that's it! The bird just chirped the answer! A five-letter word for *hopping mad* is *livid*!" Mr. Jeffers was so excited, he was spitting crumbs.

Mrs. Jeffers stopped buttering her bagel. "All I heard was chirp," she said. "Martin, you really should cut back on the coffee."

"It sounded like cheep-tweet to me," Jeremy said, shrugging his shoulders. "Dad, I think those crossword puzzles are starting to drive you batty. Maybe you should switch over to computer games. They're a whole lot tamer."

Mr. Jeffers wiped the spittle from his lips and took another sip of coffee to steady his nerves. "I'm telling you," he said, "I'm on to something here. What do you say we put this bird to the test?"

Jeremy's father prattled off question after question: four-letter word for *brown seaweed*, five-letter word for *thick slices*,

nine-letter word for *small kangaroos*—
and on and on. As he scribbled furiously
in the little squares, the budgie cheeped,
peeped, and, when things got ridiculously
easy, pecked at the dandruff in Mr. Jeffers'
hair.

Jeremy and his mother sat, dumbfounded.

"The most amazing thing," Mr. Jeffers
said, pausing long enough to shake the
kinks out of his fingers, "is how that tiny
thimble-size brain can hold so much trivial
information!"

"Really, Martin, all I hear is a chirp."

"Yeah Dad, I still say it's nothing but
cheep-tweet."

After school, Jeremy hurried home with
big plans. He was going to tape-record the
bird's chitter chatter and get to the bottom
of this once and for all. He'd ask his mother
to help. At least she wasn't all gaga over the
bird like his Dad!

But when he walked through the front
door he realized he might have been wrong.
The wild glint in his mother's eyes could
mean only one thing: Big time gaga!

"Jeremy," she gushed, bubbling with excitement, "this budgie absolutely adores the violin. I've been playing for an hour and it hasn't missed a single note." She placed the instrument on her shoulder and Beauty zoomed down from the banister for a clean landing on the bow. "Now," she said, "what do you think of this?"

As his mother began to play, Beauty balanced on the bow tip, hanging on for dear life, swooshing up and down like a crazy roller coaster ride. Was Jeremy imagining it or was the bird cheeping on the smooth strokes and tweeting on the bouncy ones? He shook his head, trying to clear his ears. There were no two ways about it—this thing should have come with a warning:

Caution.
Has potential to bring out
weirdness in parents!
Pet-sit at your own risk.

Jeremy mumbled something about an emergency at Murphy's house and sprinted out the door.

Murphy was in his backyard garden, squishing bugs on the cauliflower plants. He listened to Jeremy's sad tale.

"The same thing happened to me," he said, "when I first got my skateboard. For the whole weekend I sat on the front steps and watched my parents take turns zooming down the street. It was so embarrassing! By the time they got tired of it, I almost didn't want it anymore."

"Jeez, Murph, that's not the same thing at all," Jeremy said. "That old skateboard is still beating around your garage, but I've only got Beauty till Monday. What if Mom and Dad stay nuts till then? Will I ever have any time with her? I mean, will I?"

Murphy didn't have an answer to that.

At bedtime, Jeremy put the birdcage on his dresser, checking to make sure the seed mixture and water were topped up. Then, just as he was crawling into bed, his mother strolled into the room in search of dirty clothes. She checked here and there, peeking under the bed and poking in the Lego tub, while he pretended to be riveted

15
Library Media Center
Washington School
3 Sage Drive

to his Minky Moore book. Finally, he could stand it no longer.

"Have you seen Beauty around anywhere?" he blurted. "Is she still camped out on Dad's smelly old head?"

His mother pulled a muddy sock from the bookcase and dropped it into the laundry basket. "The bird's moved down to your father's shoulder," she said, sounding lonely. "Apparently, they're discussing the business page. What's hot and what's not."

"Business page!" shrieked Jeremy. "Minky's hotter than any old business page! His ship is stuck in ice up near Baffin Island; the only food left is peppermint nobs and bananas, and the entire crew is going snaky."

His mother gave him a helpless shrug and headed for the door with the muddy sock.

"Hey, Mom," Jeremy muttered from behind his book, "if you're so desperate for dirty clothes, check out the window ledge behind the curtain!"

Jeremy's mother was nowhere to be seen at breakfast the next morning, and since his father was busy coaxing a burnt bagel from the toaster, Jeremy had no choice but to fend for himself.

He stretched up on his tippy toes to reach his cereal bowl. "Where's Mom?" he asked. "And where's the bird?"

Mr. Jeffers looked at his watch. "They've been twenty-five minutes so far, and counting."

"Huh?"

"They're whooping it up in the shower," his father said, shaking the toaster upside down. "Your mother will be out when she runs out of songs, which should be any minute now." He tilted his head to listen. "Hear that? They're singing 'Row, Row, Row Your Boat.' Surely there can't be too many left after this!"

Jeremy watched as his father scraped the black crust off his bagel. "You and Mom really like Mrs. Flight's bird, don't you, Dad? I mean really, really like."

Mr. Jeffers didn't answer. He seemed to be staring into space. Actually, he seemed to have forgotten that Jeremy was even there.

Holy cow! thought Jeremy. His father's eyes were going all slushy and gushy.

Jeremy decided to stop asking questions and concentrate on his Cheerios. His parents were getting so wacko over that darn bird, it was giving him the creeps!

Mr. Jeffers brightened when he heard whistling and chirping coming down the hall toward the kitchen. He casually opened the paper to the crossword page and lay it next to his plate just as Mrs. Jeffers waltzed into the room. She looked like an escaped genie, what with the fat pink towel coiled around her head and the little bird jostling along on top.

"Didn't mean to use up all the hot water," she said, pouring her coffee. "But you-know-who was perched on the shower curtain rod and simply refused to quit. We sang every song we knew and then a few we didn't!" She raised her eyebrows, trying to look up. "Breakfast, my little tweety bird! Hop on down!"

Beauty gave a lively chirrup and swooped straight into the burnt bagel crumbs on the table, pecking them up like fat, juicy worms. She then skittered among the cups and plates, stopping only to have a wrestling match with a crumpled paper towel. Jeremy's parents laughed until tears rolled down their cheeks.

"I'm definitely taking a fancy to this bird," his mother said, dabbing her eyes. "What do you think, Jeremy?"

Jeremy wasn't so sure a bird was the pet for him, but it *did* seem to be the perfect pet for his parents. Perhaps he would keep searching a while longer!

Life's Not Fair!

As soon as Duffer waddled through the front door, it was love at first sight. Here was a tummy warmer and reading buddy all wrapped up in one fuzzy bundle! The hefty orange cat brushed against Jeremy's leg and purred.

"I do believe she's taking a shine to you," said Mr. Tubbs with a chuckle. "Duffer doesn't turn on the old thunder purr for just any Tom, Dick or Harry." He gave Jeremy a wink, as if he was about to share some deep secret. "A cat can sniff out a cat-person a mile off," he whispered. "It's like cat people have a special magnetic attraction and cats can't help but be drawn to them."

Jeremy crouched down and ran his hand over the thick, sturdy back. He wasn't sure about the magnet idea, but there did seem to be a touch of static in the fur.

"Don't mind the stumpy tail and mangled ears," Mr. Tubbs said. "The odd battle scar and unfortunate blemish are what give Duff her irresistible charm." He leaned down to scratch a tattered earflap. "This old girl's got a bit of history behind her. She wasn't always the pampered puss you see before you now."

Duffer responded by nudging the shopping bags Mr. Tubbs had placed on the floor.

"No, no, I won't forget to tell Jeremy about the essentials," Mr. Tubbs said, giving the heavy bags a poke with his toe. "Duffy loves her food," he explained. "Maybe a tad too much, but she's a real little beggar. Don't be surprised if she talks you into opening a third can for dessert."

Jeremy peeked into a bag and saw cans and cans of Tasty Tuna for the Finicky Feline. Duffer peeked too and, with a quick flick of the tongue over the lips, she let out a long hungry meow.

"Tut tut tut!" Mr. Tubbs scolded, tapping his watch. "Still forty-nine minutes and fifteen seconds to supper. You're not home now, you little scamp!"

Duffer twined around Jeremy's legs and twitched her stumpy tail. Jeremy was so tickled, he was speechless.

"Oh, and by the way," Mr. Tubbs said, furiously thinking of last minute reminders, "keep a teeny trickle running in the bathtub faucet. Duff gets a mite thirsty when everyone's asleep. And don't watch Channel 54 on the telly...the new weatherman sends her into fits. Oh, and she prefers her meals on bone china. Don't try to fool her with that cheap porcelain; she can tell the difference a mile off. And when the phone rings— "

"Good-bye, Mr. Tubbs."

Jeremy felt bad about shooing Mr. Tubbs out the door, but he had a feeling the poor man could rattle on for a very long time. Besides, Duffer would tell him everything he needed to know.

The cat pressed her beefy head into Jeremy's shin and meowed. He watched her for a moment, puzzled, and then his face brightened. "Oh," he said, "I get it! You want a guided tour! No, not a guided tour? You just want me to show you the sunniest, coziest spot for napping?" He laughed. "Well, follow me."

Jeremy headed for the living room while Duffer, belly swaying, tottered along behind.

"You can share my dad's special chair," Jeremy said, patting the high cushioned back. "If you stretch out up here you can see everything that happens through the window. It'll be like your own cat TV. Sound like fun?"

Duffer hopped up to test it. The view was excellent: Two black crows were playing tug-of-war with a chip bag on the sidewalk and neither one was backing down. The only thing that needed the slightest adjustment was the comfort level, but a few quick rakes with the claws made it comfy-cozy perfect. Duffer settled down for a midday nap.

"Come on, Duff, you old sleepyhead. I've still got to show you the backyard."

Duffer yawned.

"Lots of butterflies to chase," said Jeremy.

Duffer made a bouncy leap to the floor.

Mr. Jeffers was traipsing across the grass with a scraggly snowball tree in a bucket when he spotted the orange tabby. "I see Mr. Tubbs dropped off his prized pumpkin!" he said, setting the tree down. He pulled off his gardening gloves and held out his hand for a wet, sandpaper lick.

"Duffer's not a pumpkin, Dad. She's a cat, and I want one just like her!"

"How can you be so sure?" his father asked, massaging the tattered ear. "I mean, she's only just arrived."

"Magnets," said Jeremy. "We're both loaded with them."

His father gave him a quizzical look and Jeremy had a hunch that a stream of poky questions was about to come his way.

"Oops, gotta go, Dad. Gotta give The Duff a ride over to Murphy's house." He wrapped his arms around the chunky belly and off they went.

24

Murphy took one look at the mangy puff-ball bumping along in the back of the wagon and forgot all about the spider he was feeding. "Whoa, Jeremy, where'd you get the monster cat?"

"Duffer's everything I want!" Jeremy said, lifting the cat to the ground. "She belongs to Mr. Tubbs down on the corner."

Murphy knelt down for a closer inspection, trying his best to find good things to say. After all, if Jeremy really liked this tubby thing, it couldn't be *all* bad.

"I hate to tell you this," he said at last, "but have you checked out the ears? The left one is half missing! And someone stole the tail, or at least three-quarters of it." He poked around some more. "Let's see, six scars on the head, and I think this leg had a big scab once. There's no fur and the skin looks kind of funny."

Duffer backed up slowly and wedged herself between Jeremy's feet.

"I don't care what you say," Jeremy said proudly. "I've got my own tiger! Here, hop back in, Duff. We're leaving. Murph doesn't have the magnets."

"What do you mean I don't have any magnets? You know I've got magnets! You borrowed them for your science project. Remember?"

"You wouldn't understand," Jeremy said, rolling his eyes. He turned down the driveway and pulled the rattling wagon home. Duffer didn't even look back.

Jeremy stretched across his bed and flicked a mock fishing pole in the air. The feather tied to the string fluttered and flittered.

"Catch the fish, Duff," he teased, dragging the purple feather along the floor.

Duffer crouched under the desk, lurking, eyes darting this way and that. Finally, when her little cat brain told her the moment was perfect, she made a dainty, springy pounce. Jeremy gave a sharp tug and ... she missed! Jeremy giggled and Duffer crept back under the desk to begin the fun again. After four pounces, Jeremy let her hook the prey.

Duffer spit the ticklish feather out. Where were the guts and gills? The slimy, slubby scales? The heavenly, fishy taste? Jeremy had tricked her! Miffed, she hopped up on the bed.

"How about some Minky Moore?" Jeremy asked, reaching for his book. "Minky is in Egypt, digging for mummies in the desert. So far, all he's found is a whole bunch of sand."

Duffer snuggled down, crushing Jeremy's belly like a big fuzzy brick. Jeremy propped the book up on her back. "Perfect height," he mumbled. "Just don't squirm too much."

As he began reading, he watched the cat out of the corner of his eye. She seemed to be listening, so he decided to test her.

"If you think Minky should start digging in a different spot," he said, "wiggle your left ear."

It wiggled. Jeremy decided to get more personal.

"Are you the best pet in the whole world? Twitch your tail for yes."

The stumpy tail twitched. Jeremy couldn't resist digging deeper.

"Do you like me better than Mr. Tubbs?" he asked. "Shut your eyes for a count of three for yes."

Done. Jeremy held his breath and decided to go for broke.

"Do you want me to ask Mr. Tubbs if he'll trade you for that lucky baseball I found in the ditch? Roll over on your back for yes."

The roly-poly cat rolled right off his stomach, over the side of the bed, and landed belly up on the floor.

Wow! Jeremy was convinced that a miracle had just taken place.

That night, Mrs. Jeffers woke with a start.

"Ah-choo!"

She padded down the hall to Jeremy's bedroom and peeked in the doorway. "Jeremy," she whispered into the darkness, "are you awake?"

"Ah-choo!"

She flicked on the bedside lamp, and Jeremy gazed up at her with red, watery eyes. Duffer, nestled close by the pillow, batted a hairy paw across the tip of his nose every time he sneezed, snuffled or sniffled.

"I think you're coming down with a ghastly cold," his mother said, rubbing his forehead. "We'll pay a visit to Doctor Duggan first thing in the morning."

"Ah-choo!"

Doctor Duggan hummed and hawed as he stuck a Popsicle stick down Jeremy's throat. "Say aahh," he instructed. "A nice long aaaahh."

The only way for Jeremy to keep from gagging and concentrate on aahhing was to focus on the loopy mustache coiled around the doctor's mouth. It reminded him of the curvy handlebars on his bicycle.

The doctor dropped the Popsicle stick into the trash can. "There are no signs of a sore throat or high temperature," he said, slightly perplexed. "What precisely are your symptoms again?"

"Itchy lips," said Jeremy, scratching them with his teeth. "Watery eyes too. And my nose is so stuffy I have to breathe through my mouth. Oh yeah, I sneezed about a hundred and fifty times since I got up this morning. And that's not counting all the sneezes in the middle of the night."

"Hmm, interesting case." Doctor Duggan leaned back in his chair and twirled his bristly whiskers. "Now tell me, have you been exposed to anything new in your environment lately?"

"Have I what?"

Doctor Duggan adjusted his glasses. "Has anything different come into your house?" he said. "Anything out of the ordinary?"

"Uh, just Duffer."

"Duffer? Is this a new feather quilt or something?"

Jeremy laughed. "Duffer is only the best cat in the whole world," he bragged. "My friend Murph thinks he's a tubby old fur ball full of scars and scabs, but I think he's perfect."

The doctor made a strange gasping sound. Jeremy wasn't sure if he was stifling a chuckle or choking on some mustache whiskers. After a few seconds, he began again.

"Jeremy," he said solemnly, "I think I can say with nearly complete certainty that what we're dealing with here is an acute hypersensitivity."

"What does *that* mean?" Jeremy was growing tired of this doctory mumbo jumbo.

31

Doctor Duggan looked bewildered. "It means, Jeremy, that you have an allergy to cat hair. This creature will have to find another home, and your bedroom will require a thorough, all-out cleaning."

Jeremy sprang to his feet, his heart jumping and flipping in his chest. "Couldn't I wear a paper bag over my head?" he squealed. "Paper is good protective armor. I could cut out eyes and— "

It was no use. His mother shooed him out the door before he flooded the doctor in tears.

Jeremy stood on the steps and waved goodbye as Duffer's fat pumpkin-belly jiggled and wiggled down the driveway behind Mr. Tubbs. Every now and then the cat glanced back and gave a gloomy little meow. Jeremy meowed back.

Mr. Tubbs was right about the magnets, thought Jeremy, but now he had these stupid sniffles, and everything was ruined. The question was, Would he ever, in a million skillion years, find another pet as perfect as The Duff?

The Swirly-Haired Eating Machine

Jeremy was still missing Duffer when creaky Mr. McCavie shuffled up the driveway with a faded blue baby blanket cradled in his arms.

"Guinea pigs are as harmless as infants," he cooed, rocking the tiny bundle to and fro. He folded back the soft flannel and held his treasure out for inspection.

Jeremy stared at the scruffy lump of twisty gray hair. "Which end is the head?" he asked. "And doesn't it have any legs?"

"Guinea's hunched down having a little snooze, that's all," said Mr. McCavie. "Plop him anywhere, and he'll be happy as a clam."

Jeremy crossed his fingers. Maybe Guinea *would* be the perfect replacement for Duffer—he sure looked cuddly with all that long swirly hair. So what if he acted as lively as a doorstop? It was probably because old Mr. McCavie hadn't read him any good adventure stories lately.

"Likes to nibble now and then, but he's a smart little fellow," Mr. McCavie said. "He knows what's important and what's not, so no need to worry there." The old man tickled the guinea pig under the chin, and it raised its head and chittered.

"There, there, Guin, my little ragamuffin. Papa will be back to get you in a few days. You listen to your uncle Jeremy now. He'll load you up on cucumber and parsley and anything else your heart desires."

"Chit, chit, chitter! Chitter, chitter, chit!" Guinea had plenty to say.

Mr. McCavie leaned forward, hand to his ear. Finally, he wagged a wobbly finger and scolded, "Now don't go telling me one of your silly jokes if you're going to keep the punch line to yourself!"

Guinea scuttled into a fold in the blanket and hid.

"He knows what's happening here," Mr. McCavie said with a sigh. "And the wee thing is trying to ease the situation with a bit of humor. Oh, my nerves, this is hard for me. Best to get it over with quickly." He placed the bundle in Jeremy's arms, gave his nose a quick flick and shuffled back down the driveway.

Jeremy found his mother in the kitchen with her rear end sticking out of the musty cupboard under the sink.

"Pass me that plumbers' wrench," she said, flapping her hand in the air. "We've got a major drip down here."

Jeremy passed his mother the wrench and watched her plaid bum wiggle as she worked. "Old Mr. McCavie from over on Tupper Street just dropped off a pet," he said. "Want to see?"

"Hang on a few more seconds," said his mother. "This ancient plumbing needs a bit of coaxing." After a few loud bangs, thuds and grunts, she crawled out from the maze of pipes. "That should do it," she said, snapping the toolbox shut. "Now, Jeremy, let's see what it is you have there."

Jeremy sat on the floor, lifted the timid creature out of its nest and handed it to his mother. Her eyes sparkled. "Good heavens!" she cried. "It's shaped like a corncob, only bushy!" She snuggled the little critter into her neck. "But Jeremy, about all this whirly hair … I'm a bit concerned."

"No runny nose yet," he said sniffing deeply, "not even a sneeze."

While his mother got acquainted with the guinea pig, Jeremy needed a few things cleared up, but he wasn't sure how to begin.

"Uh, Mom, how come … how come Mr. McCavie looks so … so …"

His mother stood Guinea up on his hind legs and inspected his pudgy tummy. "So what?" she asked. "How come Mr. McCavie looks so what?"

"So … so … shabby. You ever notice his choppy hair, all patchy and everything. He's almost bald near his left ear." Jeremy tried not to laugh. "It looks like he gave himself a haircut with a knife and fork."

His mother was busy searching for a tail that didn't exist, so Jeremy kept talking.

"And his buttons, or the spots where his buttons *should* be, just have wispy dangles of thread poking out. What happened to the buttons? And how come his coat is covered in holes, trillions of tiny little holes, especially on the front?"

Guinea squeaked with joy as Mrs. Jeffers massaged and tickled his ears. "Mr. McCavie is a kindly old man, and I suspect he enjoys wearing what's comfortable," she said softly. "You know, Jeremy, sometimes the older people get the less importance they place on appearances. This little guy is the center of Mr. McCavie's world. A few missing buttons don't mean a thing."

That's just how I want to be with my own pet, thought Jeremy. He scooped the scruffy lump out of his mother's arms and headed off to introduce Guinea to his favorite television program.

Soon after Mr. Jeffers came home from work, he summoned Jeremy to the living room.

"What's this?" he demanded.

It was probably Jeremy's imagination, but he thought he saw puffs of smoke blowing out of his father's ears. "Jeepers, Dad, it's the TV remote. Everyone knows that!"

"Yes, I *know* it's the remote, but can you explain what happened to the knobs? There are no numbers, no arrows, no markings of any kind."

Jeremy looked more closely and knew he had some serious explaining to do. Every single knob was etched with tiny teeth marks.

"I guess Guinea got bored when we were watching Wonky Willy," he mumbled.

"I guess that about sums it up," his father fumed. He tapped the arm of his big comfy chair, as if counting to ten. "And where, may I ask, is this creature now?"

Jeremy shrugged. "I spotted him scampering down the hall a few minutes ago."

Mr. Jeffers leaned forward. "Didn't he come with some sort of a cage?"

Jeremy had a sneaky suspicion that his sunny day was about to turn cloudy. "Mr. McCavie didn't mention anything about a cage," he said, thinking quickly. "I think

Guinea's on his holidays too and wants a break from the regular routine; you know, something like summer vacation."

Mr. Jeffers grunted. "I'll let it pass this time," he huffed. "But if that guinea pig shows signs of eating us out of house and home, it'll be a clump of hay in a cardboard box for him!"

Murphy dropped by after supper to see what Jeremy had been raving about on the phone. Mr. Jeffers immediately banished them to Jeremy's bedroom.

"Zero noise," he warned. "And that means no pillow fights or roughhousing. I'm giving an important presentation tomorrow, and I'll be up half the night crunching numbers." He waved a stack of papers in the air. "These charts and graphs must be perfect!"

The boys bolted up the stairs with Guinea bouncing along in the crook of Murphy's arm. Jeremy dove for the beanbag chair and Murphy stretched out on the bed. He plunked the little animal onto his chest and began making clicking sounds with his tongue.

"Murph, what are you doing?"

Murphy giggled. "Having a person-to-piggy conversation," he said. "You just have to know the lingo."

Guinea took a timid step forward, put a paw on Murphy's chin and peered into his face with coal black eyes. Murphy blew a poof of soft breath, and Guinea's little whiskers went all of a twitch.

"Say, Jeremy, how about you nip down to the kitchen and get a nice crunchy carrot. I have a feeling there's a bit of Bugs in this guy. Have you seen the length of these teeth?"

Jeremy was still coming down the hall when Guinea's nose caught the first tantalizing whiff. In a split second, faster than it takes to say, "swish," the little creature had worked himself into a frenzy. Jeremy lay the treat on Murphy's stomach, and Guinea pounced on it, attacking it from every angle, munching loudly. Carrot crumbs flew wild.

Murphy watched in fascination. "This guy's a regular eating machine! Jeremy, you have definitely got to get one of these for your own!"

By the time the carrot was a ragged stub, it was time for Murphy to head home. He gave Guinea one last tickle under the chin and lifted the little animal off his stomach.

"Arrrgh!" he screamed, eyes wide. "What're those?"

Dozens of teeny brown pellets littered his belly.

"It's...uh...uh...it's..." Jeremy was having trouble getting his words out.

"Pooh!" Murphy screamed again, hopping to his feet. "That thing pooped all over me! Gross! I'll be dreaming about this all night!"

As he tugged and pulled at his clothes, he glared at Jeremy. "Stop your laughing," he grumbled. "It's not funny!"

At bedtime, Jeremy snuggled under the covers, happy that everything was going his way. His favorite baseball pajamas were warm and fluffy, straight from the hot dryer. *The Adventures of Minky Moore in Singapore*, his new library book, was sure to keep him reading way past nine o'clock. And, best of all, a fuzzy, gray lump murmured away on his chest, on top of an old towel—just in case.

Jeremy peered into its dark eyes. "Say, Guin, don't you ever blink?"

Guinea's nose twitched.

"Well, hang on to your socks," Jeremy said, opening the book. "Minky is gonna be so exciting, I probably won't do a whole lot of blinking either."

The little guinea pig listened attentively, but by the third chapter it found itself with the book on its head and Jeremy snoring away on the pillow.

In the morning, Jeremy's perfect world was not so perfect anymore. He awoke to discover the buttons on his favorite pajamas missing and the bed covered in shredded paper. Poor Minky had turned into a tasty night time snack!

Jeremy scrambled to gather the chewed scraps of paper, thinking that maybe he could tape them all back together, but it soon became clear that the best parts were deep inside Guinea's stomach. He flopped down on the bed, woozy with worry. "That

was a library book!" he cried. "Do you know the trouble I'm in now?"

Guinea looked up with an innocent gaze.

When Jeremy trudged downstairs for breakfast, he had to give his eyes a good rub to make sure he was awake. It wasn't every morning his father danced and twirled around the kitchen with a briefcase so bulging with papers that they poked out in all directions.

Mr. Jeffers let out a yowl and slid into his chair like it was home base. "My big presentation is finished," he said, pleased as punch. "In fact, it's picture perfect. The charts and graphs are outstanding." He reached across the table and stabbed a stack of pancakes. "Nothing like a late night of number crunching to work up a hearty appetite!"

"That's wonderful," Mrs. Jeffers said. "Don't you think that's wonderful, Jeremy?"

Jeremy nodded and concentrated on picking the blueberries out of his pancakes. What was really wonderful, he thought, was that his father seemed to have forgotten all about the chewed knobs on the TV remote, especially now that he had a bit of explaining to do about the library book.

Mr. Jeffers was about to smother his pancakes in syrup when he stopped with the bottle in midair. He looked perplexed. "Jeremy," he said, studying his son. "There's something different about you this morning. Why, it's the hair! Have you been snipping it with the nail clippers?"

That evening, Mr. Jeffers marched through the front door with a cardboard box in his arms and a nasty scowl on his face. Jeremy was pretty sure the puffs of ear smoke were back too.

"Jeremy Reginald Jeffers!"

Jeremy swallowed a lump the size of a frog and headed downstairs with the guinea pig in his arms. His father only used his full name when he was in a whole whack of trouble.

"See this box? See all this nice cozy hay? See that guinea pig?"

Jeremy thought his father sounded a bit weird, but he nodded anyway.

"*That* animal goes into *this* box," his father said, "and there it stays until its little visit is over!"

Then he held up his briefcase. "Do you know what's in here?"

Jeremy wanted to look at the briefcase, but his eyes remained glued to the toes of his father's shiny black shoes.

"This is what *used* to be my professional presentation," his father roared. "The same one I slaved over until the early hours of the morning. The one with all the picture-perfect charts and graphs. But when I pulled it out during my meeting, it was ruined...shredded...savaged with tiny teeth marks. Instead of amazing and astounding all those important clients, do you know what happened instead?"

Jeremy thought it best to maintain total silence.

Mr. Jeffers collapsed into his comfy chair as if all the strength had been zapped from his legs.

"I stuttered and stammered," he said

46

glumly. "I bumbled and fumbled. I don't know if anyone believed my harebrained excuse about an out-of-control guinea pig who thinks he's on summer vacation."

Jeremy skulked upstairs. He hoped that Guinea wouldn't let on to Mr. McCavie that he had to spend his last night of vacation huddled in a lonely cardboard box.

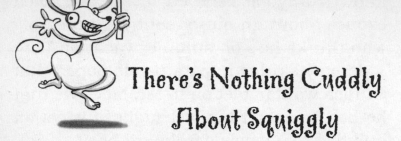

There's Nothing Cuddly About Squiggly

When Jeremy's principal offered to let him fish-sit for the weekend, Jeremy wasn't sure. He wanted a pet—that was certain—but how cuddly and playful could two slippery, squiggly little goldfish be?

"They'll give you hours of delight," said Mr. Gill, plunking the aquarium on the coffee table with a thud. Water sloshed over the carpet, and he sheepishly kicked off a shoe and blotted it up with the toe of his sock before getting down to business.

"The big, burly brute is Mac, and the wee, delicate one is Cheese," Mr. Gill said proudly. He stepped back to admire the two shiny shapes that were gliding this way and that. "You'll soon discover they've each got their own charms and personalities. But Jeremy, for heaven's sake, don't pay too much attention to Cheese—you know, goggling and winking at him through the glass, or Mac will get jealous and sulk down around the ferns. Might not see him for days! We don't want that now, do we?"

Jeremy shook his head.

"Give them a pinch of food at breakfast and another pinch at supper. Not too much, mind you, just an eensy-weensy smidgen. A little fish's stomach is no bigger than its eyeball, and too much food can have some mighty unpleasant consequences!"

Mr. Gill's eyebrows knit together in one long black fuzzy stretch. Jeremy knew that the principal was gearing up to say something serious. "I don't want to find my little darlings floating belly-up on Monday morning," he warned. "Nothing but top-notch health will do."

Jeremy gulped and tried his best to look interested as Mr. Gill unfolded a long list of instructions, perched his glasses on the tip of his nose, and began.

"Check the tank often," he instructed.

"Conduct a proper head count every day, several times a day if necessary. Make sure there are two at all times. Mac is a bit of a daredevil and thinks it's fun to escape. Jumps clear across the floor..." Mr. Gill's voice trailed off, and he dabbed his eyes with a wrinkly hanky. "He doesn't know the dangers, lad. Thinks the whole world is one big friendly ocean."

The principal waited a moment to control his sniffles and then continued. "Check for gasping at the surface or sinking to the bottom," he said, glancing up to make sure Jeremy was heeding every word. "And keep a sharp eye out for any hint of disease—dots, slime, fuzz, rot and whatnot—that's all a sure sign of trouble."

Jeremy's head went dizzy as the big man rattled on. The scribbles seemed to go on forever: bubbling bubblers, algae scrub pads, thermometer checks, water testing, chlorine drops. How was he going to keep it all straight?

"Now, listen up!" Mr. Gill's fuzzy eyebrows did a funny little dance. "What I'm about to tell you is crucial."

Jeremy snapped to attention.

"Mac will only eat with the light on, but Cheese is a bit finicky. He'll only eat with the light off. Do your best to keep it all straight, lad! Keeping fish is a complicated, ticklish business." Mr. Gill attempted a rather squishy wink. "Not everyone has the delicate touch," he said, "but I have great faith in you."

As his car backed down the driveway, Mr. Gill poked his head out the window. "My emergency number is written right there on the instruction sheet," he shouted. "Telephone me if anything seems out of whack, anything at all. I'll fly home immediately."

Jeremy had a sinking feeling in his stomach. This was way too confusing to handle alone. He needed Murphy.

The next morning, Jeremy was dawdling over breakfast, worrying about his first fish feeding, when Murphy showed up to offer assistance. He had written a school report on guppies last year and now considered himself an expert on anything with fins, gills and scales.

Murphy inspected the little can of fish food. "Brine shrimp flakes," he read. "Guaranteed to meet the special dietary requirements of all your aquarium fish." He opened the lid and sniffed.

"Gross me out!" he cried. "I sucked some right up my nose!"

Jeremy laughed. "Yeah, and I think I see a big slimy fin sprouting out of the top of your head!"

They hobbled to the living room in hysterics.

Then things got serious.

Jeremy tried to keep his hand steady as he held the food can over the open aquarium. All he could think about was Mr. Gill's crusty face and his million-and-one instructions.

"Careful, now," said Murphy. "The instructions say a light sprinkle. Actually, maybe you should shake a bit in your hand first, just to make sure you don't overdo it."

"Jeepers, Murph, I know what I'm doing!" Jeremy gave the can a light tap on the side of the tank.

"Oh, no! Oh, my gosh! Oh, no!"

They watched in horror as every last flake tumbled out of the can and sank effortlessly to the bottom. Mac and Cheese turned into faint glints of gold, disappearing in the murky water.

Jeremy's lip quivered. "They'll eat like little pigs till they burst!" he sputtered. "Mr. Gill is gonna be mad as heck! He'll have me be scrubbing the gym floor with my toothbrush!"

"Quick, go get your dad!"

"I can't. He might think I'm not responsible!" Jeremy stirred the water around with his finger. "Holy Moly, Mac is already looking puffy and bloated! How long does it take before he blows up altogether?"

Murphy frantically tried to remember his guppy project and wished now that he had paid closer attention. "We gotta rescue them," he said finally. "It's not eating too much that'll kill them, it's all that mucky water. We have to take the old water out and put clean stuff back in. And it has to be the right temperature—not too warm and not too cool."

Panic-stricken, Jeremy raced to the kitchen and returned laden with emergency supplies. He handed Murphy a soup ladle.

"Here, poke around until you find them," he said. "Drop them in my cereal bowl for safe keeping. I'll scoop the dirty water into Mom's mixing bowl."

"Hey, isn't that your father's coffee mug, the one you gave him for his birthday?"

Jeremy looked at the chunky blue mug with *40 Ain't Old if You're a Tree* stamped on the front in bold red letters. "Yeah, but this is life-or-death," he said, dipping as fast as he could. "And besides, Dad will never know!"

After what seemed like an eternity, with Mac and Cheese waiting patiently in the cereal bowl, the tank was finally emptied. Jeremy refilled it with sparkling clean water, squirted in a few chlorine drops and dropped the fish back into their home. They went right back to their usual games—skittering through the ferns playing hide-and-seek, and nipping each other's tail in tag, you're it.

"Dad!" Jeremy had been holding his breath so long he hadn't noticed his father coming into the room.

"Oh, there it is! Strange ... I don't remember

leaving it here." Mr. Jeffers picked up his mug from the coffee table. "I'll just nip out, pour a cup and be right back."

Jeremy's stomach did a flip-flop.

Murphy's face went pasty.

Should they confess about the mug?

Too late. Mr Jeffers was already back with the steamy mug, settling into his chair and taking his first germy sip.

"Peaceful creatures, aren't they?" he said, admiring the crystal clear aquarium. "A bit weak in the brain department, but no trouble at all to care for. Hmmm..." He stared into his mug and frowned. "There's a peculiar taste to this coffee. I must ask your mother if she's been experimenting with a new flavor."

Jeremy and Murphy quickly escaped outside.

Since the food can was now empty, Mac and Cheese had to do without for the rest of the weekend. If they were really starving, Jeremy figured that they could nibble the edge of a tasty fern or lick the scuzz off the slimy pebbles.

When Monday morning rolled around, Mr. Gill rang the doorbell before Jeremy had even brushed his teeth. "Came to pick up my little darlings early to squeeze in some quality time before school," he said, rushing into the living room. "My, my, don't they look sprightly! I've never seen Cheese so playful! Look at him, darting around like he's king of the tank!" He slapped Jeremy on the back and chuckled. "Jeremy, my boy, you'll be a proud pet owner yourself, soon enough. Consider an aquarium, lad. It's not hard to tell you have natural talent as a fish-keeper."

Jeremy managed a weak smile. He was glad the principal could not hear the thumpety-thumping of his heart. Mr. Gill had no idea how close he had come to being fishless this morning!

The minute Mac and Cheese flicked their golden tails goodbye, Jeremy slammed the door shut and took a big gulp of air. Fish were definitely at the very bottom of his pet wish list.

Pet-Sitting on School Property

Mrs. Roden stood in the doorway clutching a small metal cage. "Allow me to introduce you to Frisket," she said.

Jeremy peered inside at an itsy-bitsy food bowl, a water bottle, a shiny silver wheel and, piled up in one corner, a messy mound of cedar shavings and cottony fluff.

"Did he escape?"

Mrs. Roden chuckled. "Hamsters don't like being woken from their naps," she said, pointing to the messy burrow. "They're sleepy little critters in the daytime but barrels of fun at night...you'll see!" She thrust the cage into his arms. "Give him lots of treats so he won't miss me so much. Dates and walnuts make dandy snacks, but don't feed him too much—he tends to squirrel food away in every nook and cranny."

And with that, Mrs. Roden waved a hasty toodle-oo and trotted off down the street. Jeremy glanced down at the cage and shook his head. He did feel a tiny bit foolish going inside to show off a pet he couldn't see.

He found his parents up to their eyeballs making apple pies.

His mother was attacking a stiff lump of dough with a rolling pin, trying to coax it into a thin, round circle. And his father was looking none too happy with the grim task of peeling, peeling and more peeling. His face lit up when Jeremy plunked the little cage on the table. He pushed the apple basket aside and leaned in for a closer look.

"And what do we have here?" he asked. "A mystery pet?"

"A hamster," Jeremy said, slumping down into a chair. "Mrs. Roden said he was a barrel of fun, but I've got my doubts. I mean, jeepers, what good is a pet who has his days and nights mixed up?"

His mother ran her doughy fingers across

the bars of the cage. "It can't be easy being nocturnal," she said. "All those long, lonely nights...the whole house asleep...no one paying the slightest attention to you..."

"Mom, watch it! You're flicking flour and bits of gook over everything. Frisket might be allergic to it or something!"

Mrs. Jeffers smiled and went back to rolling dough.

"I had a hamster when I was about your age," his father said wistfully. "I loved that little rascal to pieces. He could even charm the socks off the mailman, what with those chubby cheeks and all."

"Yeah, well, at least you got to play with him," Jeremy grumbled. "I don't even know what Frisket looks like."

Mr. Jeffers dangled a strip of apple peel over the messy nest. "Let's see if this gets his nose twitching. My little Hammy would snap wide awake if there was the tiniest whiff of fruit in the air."

Jeremy held his breath and waited, but all he glimpsed through a hole in the bedding was a snippet of white fur—and that snippet showed no signs of stirring.

His face drooped. It would take more than the thrill of apple peel to bring this little guy to his taps.

"You know, Jeremy," his father said, "if he's going to snooze all day, why not take him to school? A hamster can sleep in a shirt pocket as well as he can in his cage. At least it would give you a chance to spend some time together."

The rolling pin clattered to the floor. "Martin, where do you come up with these crazy notions? A caper like that could land poor Jeremy in a whole heap of trouble."

"Fiddlesticks!" said Mr. Jeffers. "It's one hundred percent foolproof. If Frisket won't stir for a juicy strip of apple peel, it's a safe bet he won't get too hyped up over times-tables."

Jeremy couldn't believe that this was his father talking, especially after all the goings on with the guinea pig.

"Be sure to tuck a few tissues in the pocket, Jeremy, for an extra degree of coziness."

"Martin!"

Something told Jeremy that this might be a good time for a hasty exit. He grabbed the cage and scooted upstairs. No matter what his mother said, he had made up his mind: A pocket pet might be the best pet of all! And heck, even though there was a no-pet rule at school, Miss Mudd would never know, for during the day, little Frisket was invisible.

That night, just as Jeremy was hopping into his pajamas, Frisket was crawling out of his messy mound, ready to start a busy day. Jeremy lay on his bed with the cage balanced on his stomach and watched as the hamster got down to the critical task of washing and sprucing up. It looked like he was wearing a furry white snowsuit with teeny pink gloves, matching pink toe-socks and dainty pink ears sticking out of the hood ... and every single spec had to be scrubbed until it sparkled.

"You're coming to school with me tomorrow," Jeremy said softly. "Miss Mudd, that's my teacher, she's got this singsong voice that'll knock you right out." He stuck his finger between the bars for a get-acquainted sniff. "You can curl up in my shirt pocket and snooze up a storm."

The little hamster clenched its teeny pink fists and had a monstrous stretch.

Jeremy grinned. He just knew that Frisket was saying, Yippee!

"You want to hear about Minky diving in the Caribbean?" Jeremy asked, reaching for his book on the night table. "Minky's found this pirate ship that sank in 1792. Think of what you could do with all that gold, Frisky...a triple-decker cage, a slew of toys, maybe even a little buddy for company!"

Frisket rose up on his hind legs, nose high in the air, ears alerted to the rustling pages. Jeremy took this as a sign that he had a true-blue Minky Moore fan on his hands.

But it was not to be, for Jeremy had barely reached the third word when the little hamster hopped into his silver wheel and began his nightly marathon, mile after squeaky mile.

Jeremy groaned, pulled his pillow over his head and fell into a fretful sleep.

At school the next day, Miss Mudd squinted into her teacup. "What's this?" she asked, tilting the cup for the class to see. "Did someone lose a furry white pom-pom?"

The little pom-pom stirred and enjoyed a lazy, toothy yawn.

"EEEK!"

Jeremy's stomach tumbled to his sneakers. He tapped his shirt pocket: Empty!

"EEEK! EEEK!"

The teacup shattered into a million pieces, and a furry white blur bolted for safety under the bookcase.

Miss Mudd clutched her chest and her breaths came out in strange, raspy spurts. "Which one of you is responsible for this...this joke...this prank...this..." All the EEEKING seemed to have eeeked the words from her throat.

The entire class sat with their chins on their chests. It wasn't every day that sweet, sugary Miss Mudd sputtered foam and bellowed like a mad thing!

"Someone had better step forward," she shrieked, "and they had better make it snappy!"

Jeremy glanced over at Murphy, hoping for support, but Murphy was slinking down

in his seat, trying to disappear. Jeremy was on his own! Oh well, he thought, if Minky could weasel out of dicey situations, so could he. He pushed himself to his feet.

Miss Mudd waggled a shaky finger in his direction. "Retrieve that rodent and off you go!" she roared. "Off, Off, Off! Take it and march right down to the principal's office!"

Trembling, Jeremy crouched down on his knees, peered under the bookcase and scooped the frightened hamster up. With Frisket cupped in his hands, he left the classroom and trudged toward the heavy brown door at the end of corridor.

Mr. Gill glared down at Jeremy in his stern principal way. "Let's get to the bottom of this, lad," he said, rubbing his wiggly chin. "When Miss Mudd ordered you to pay me a visit, how many 'offs' did she say, exactly? That's the key, you see. That's what I need to know."

Jeremy stared at the floor and tried not to cry.

"You must have a keen memory for the

finer detail," said Mr. Gill, clearly befuddled. "Miss Mudd has her own system, and that tells me the seriousness of the crime. She yells one 'off' for note passing, two 'offs' for spitballs—you get what I'm saying here, lad. All punishment hinges on you remembering the correct number of 'offs.'"

Jeremy felt giddy. It was hard to think straight when his head was jumbled.

"Four," he mumbled at last. "I think it was four. She said, 'Off you go. Off, Off, Off.'"

Mr. Gill stepped back in alarm, and his fuzzy eyebrows did their famous joining act. "Four 'offs' is serious stuff indeed," he scolded. "What sort of shenanigans were you up to anyway? I understand from the secretary that our poor Miss Mudd is still gasping for air in the staff room. Says the whole experience has her contemplating early retirement."

Jeremy stretched open his shirt pocket. "Pet business," he said. "Frisket escaped."

"Pet-sitting on school property! My, my, you *are* taking your duties seriously!" Mr. Gill bent over to tickle the sleepy ball of fur. "You know, lad, we may teach the three R's at school, but the fourth R, Responsibility, you're learning all on your own."

Jeremy wasn't sure if he should say anything, so he kept quiet.

Mr. Gill paced his office floor, stepping over piles of boxes and books, as he tried to sort out his dilemma. "There's no doubt your intentions were good," he said briskly, "but not everyone is as smitten with nature's creatures as you and I are. I'm afraid you'll have to leave the dear wee one at home from now on."

Mr. Gill planted himself on the edge of his desk and began furiously cleaning his spectacles with the tip of his necktie. "Miss Mudd is a first-rate teacher, and we like to keep her happy," he said, spitting ever so lightly on the lenses. "And now there is the little matter of the appropriate punishment. Since I've been principal, I've never had an offence of this nature."

Oh please, thought Jeremy, not the toothbrush and the gym floor!

As Mr. Gill racked his brain, his eyebrows scooted off madly in all directions— they were practically doing somersaults.

"An essay would be the perfect thing," he said at last. "The benefits of fish, to be precise. Throw in the word 'tranquillity' and I'll even print it in the school newsletter."

Jeremy looked skeptical, but Mr. Gill was growing more and more boisterous, his hands flicking and flapping like sheets in the wind.

"We have to spread the word, Jeremy, my boy! Educate your fellow students! I can't carry the burden alone. Hamsters are nice, but do you really want a pet with its snooze schedule in reverse? Go back to fish, lad. Their enthusiasm for life is infectious! No lolling around all day, catching forty winks." He tapped his suit pocket lovingly. "Oh, how I wish I could keep my little darlings here next to my heart!"

When, fifteen minutes later, the principal was still yammering on, Jeremy tiptoed out the door. He thought he had made a perfect escape, when a loud voice thundered down the hall: "Before you take one step farther, lad, secure the button on that shirt pocket!"

That evening there were no smiles or chuckles around the supper table; Miss Mudd's nippy phone call had made certain of that. Jeremy swirled his mashed potatoes around with his fork. Why do teachers only blab the bad stuff? he wondered. Last week, when he had stayed after school to help take down all the rainforest projects, Miss Mudd hadn't rushed to the phone to report *that* to his parents!

"Is that agreed then, Jeremy?"

Jeremy looked up. He hadn't been listening.

"The hamster stays home," his mother repeated. "School is off-limits to that little guy for the rest of his visit."

Jeremy gave his potatoes a final stab and pushed his plate away. "Makes no difference," he grumbled. "Jeez, what good is a pet who sleeps all day anyway? Does that sound normal to you?"

"You do get to play with him before bedtime," his father said, patting his hand.

"Not much!" cried Jeremy. "I try to get him to stay on my lap, but before I know it his butt is sticking out of my pencil holder!

Even worse, he doesn't seem to like adventure books. I don't think he's even *heard* of Minky Moore. Can you believe anything as crazy as that?"

Mr. and Mrs. Jeffers shook their heads sympathetically.

A hamster, Jeremy decided, might be great for a kid who was a night owl, but it was not the pet for him. He wasn't at all sad when Mrs. Roden's little barrel of fun toodled off home.

Drowning in Slobber

The swish of the thick, bushy tail toppled Jeremy over backwards. He looked up to see a hulking black shape towering over him. Out of its mouth dangled the longest, wettest tongue he had ever seen. Yikes! This dog was the size of a bear!

"His tail packs a strong wallop, but his heart is as gentle as a kitten," Mr. Barkley said, helping Jeremy to his feet. "Cuddles, say hello to Jeremy, your new friend."

Cuddles promptly splattered Jeremy's foot with a squishy blob of drool.

"Yecch! Gross!" Jeremy gave his foot a shake, but the sticky slime didn't budge.

Mr. Barkley threw back his head and let out a hearty laugh. "Don't worry, my boy, that's the only nasty habit my widdle cuddly-pooh has. By tomorrow, I guarantee you'll be so much in love you won't even notice the odd slobber!" Mr. Barkley scratched Cuddles' back, and the big dog swayed its massive head from side to side. A long string of drool flicked off and zinged Jeremy on the cheek.

"I've left his food out there on the curb," Mr. Barkley said, pointing to a king-size bag of chow. "I'd lug it all the way in, but the back has been acting up lately. Perhaps you wouldn't mind heaving it in your wagon and dragging it inside before the whole thing gets infested with ants."

Jeremy wiped his brow and tried to stay calm. His shoulders sagged under the heavy burden of responsibility.

"My Cuddles has a sensitive stomach," Mr. Barkley went on, "and he insists on that outlandishly expensive lamb and rice concoction. Turns his nose up at everything else, don't you, my widdle sweetness?" He leaned over for a drippy dog kiss, but instead, Cuddles banged his head into Mr. Barkley's thigh. The jolt caused the poor man to teeter and nearly crash into Jeremy.

"Oh, you little scallywag!" Mr. Barkley howled until his chins jiggled and danced. "Don't mind that little bit of rough play," he said, fumbling with the knot on a big duffel bag. "This dog is a puppy-kindergarten graduate with top honors in obedience and manners!"

He reached into the bag and pulled out two grungy bowls, a blanket, and a furry yellow duck with a bright orange beak. The beak, Jeremy noticed, was only hanging on by a few brave threads.

"Cuddles won't sleep without his comfy Bow-Wow blanket," Mr Barkley said. He handed Jeremy a tattered gray rag covered in dog hair and smelling faintly of pee. "Toss it on the floor and plop Quackers on top. But remember—if *that* duck is not with *that* blanket, there'll not be a moment's sleep for anyone! My widdle snookums is absolutely addicted to his Quackers."

Jeremy took the lumpy stuffed duck, still sticky with slobber, and let it fall to the ground with the blanket.

Mr. Barkley gave Cuddles one last bear hug and was off, leaving Jeremy and the big dog eyeball to eyeball on the porch steps. Jeremy took a deep breath. Last week he had trouble controlling a teensy pocket pet, and now he was staring into the flaring wet nostrils of a moving mountain! He tugged on the leash and dragged the humongous mutt inside.

Jeremy began by washing out one of the grungy bowls and filling it with water. That was easy. So far, so good.

"Jeremy!"

It was his mother's voice, and it sounded suspiciously shrill.

"Get into the living room this instant!"

Jeremy scrambled at once.

His mother was standing over a glob of gooey chocolatey something on the carpet, and he could tell right off the bat that she was as mad as heck.

"Any inkling as to what this might be?" she snapped.

Jeremy was dumbfounded. He didn't have the foggiest idea. He knew he should say something, even if it *was* only gibberish, but before he could speak, big burly Cuddles lumbered out from behind the sofa. A mangled, chocolate-bunny box was clenched in his jaws and brown goo dribbled from his mouth.

"Oh, oh, oh," was all Jeremy's mother could say. She wobbled a bit, and for a split second Jeremy was afraid she might topple headfirst into the brown mush.

"I'm dog-sitting for Mr. Barkley," Jeremy said quickly. "Looks like Cuddles found that Peter Cottontail I lost at Easter." He stared down at the glob. "Guess he's not a big chocolate fan."

Mrs. Jeffers slumped down on the coffee table. "You mean that…that…*thing* is just a dog?" she gasped. "Thank goodness!"

By the time Mr. Jeffers arrived home from work, Cuddles had officially adopted the big comfy chair in the living room as his own little hangout. By trial and error, he discovered that if he hung his head over one overstuffed arm and slung his rump over the other, it was the perfect fit.

Mr. Jeffers coughed to get the dog's

attention. "Uh, doggy," he said nicely. "Perhaps Jeremy neglected to inform you, but that chair you're wedged into like a sausage is mine, and I'm not in the mood to share."

Cuddles shifted his glassy black eye-balls to gaze up at the stranger.

This man didn't *look* like Mr. B.

He didn't *smell* like Mr. B.

He didn't *sound* like Mr. B.

And Mr. B. *never* walked around with a funny-looking mug.

Cuddles snuggled down to continue his dream.

Mr. Jeffers prodded the dog with his newspaper.

No response.

Mr. Jeffers prodded again, harder this time. Cuddles twisted over onto his back and lifted a hind leg as if to say, Don't stop … go for a belly scratch … a touch to the left, and a little more pressure.

"Oh, for heavens sake!" Mr. Jeffers flopped down on the stiff couch, glared over at the mangy lump, and muttered, "I don't suppose you'd care to tell me how long we'll be blessed with your delightful company?"

Cuddles answered by expelling some rather nasty vapors and draping a big slappy paw over his nose.

At bedtime, Cuddles watched as Jeremy spread the ratty old Bow-Wow blanket on his bedroom floor and carefully smoothed out the wrinkles. Jeremy placed the yellow duck on top and stepped back to study the arrangement. "Does that look about right?" he asked.

Cuddles didn't answer. Taking that to mean yes, Jeremy climbed into bed. He flicked on his lamp, reached for Minky Moore and began reading aloud. All throughout Minky's harrowing escape from flying arrows in the jungles of the Amazon, Cuddles remained frozen. Not a twitch. Not a blink. Not a fidget.

Jeremy decided to investigate. He lay the book on his lap. "Do you know where the Amazon is?" he asked.

The woebegone look on the big dog's face gave no clues.

Jeremy probed further. "Do you even *know* about Minky Moore?"

Still nothing, but an awfully big puddle of drool was building up around Cuddles' feet.

"Cuddles," Jeremy asked, "do you even *like* adventure stories?"

Cuddles pawed his blankie and whined.

"Oh, I give up!" said Jeremy, letting Minky drop to the floor. "Good night!"

He flicked off the light and was just getting cozy in the poofy softness when—

"Cuddles, get off, you mutt! You're smushing me! I can't breathe!"

Jeremy pushed as hard as he could, but Cuddles seemed to have grown onto the bed.

"What about your smelly old blanket," Jeremy cried, "the one you can't sleep without? And how did you get a name like Cuddles in the first place? You're about as cuddly as a stump!"

Cuddles nuzzled in closer, hogging what he could of the pillow, the blanket and every inch of space.

It wasn't long before Jeremy was nudged off the bed completely. He landed in the drooly puddle with a thump. There he spent a shivery night huddled on the ratty Bow-Wow blanket with Quackers bunched up under his head as a pillow. Every now and then the bushy tail swooshed down over the side of the bed, tickling his feet and sprinkling him with floating wisps of doggy hair.

At breakfast, more quirks and perks were revealed.

Drooling, it turned out, was only one of Cuddles' many special talents. Slurping water from the toilet bowl ranked a close second. And it mattered not a pinch that the lid was kept down—the big dog expertly hoisted it up with his nose. Then, after downing the very last lip-smacking drop, he sauntered into the kitchen, pitched into a shaking frenzy and splattered the entire family with slobber.

"Get that beast out of here!" Mr. Jeffers growled, gritting his teeth. "My boiled eggs are floating!"

Mrs. Jeffers frowned into her coffee cup. "Ruined," she moaned, "positively ruined!"

"Too soggy to eat!" Jeremy cried, pushing his plate away. "You know, Cuddles, you ate my chocolate bunny and then you threw up my chocolate bunny, you kicked me out of bed, and now you've ruined my toast! Mr. Barkley should have named you Trouble!"

"Trouble Smubble," Mr. Jeffers muttered. "I vote for renaming him Nuisance!"

"Uh, Jeremy," Mrs. Jeffers piped in, "maybe this would be the ideal time to take Cuddles for his morning walk. And, by all means, dawdle all you want!"

Poor Jeremy was towed along as Mr. Barkley's widdle cuddly-pooh charged full speed ahead, determined to water every tree and bush on the block. Duffer scampered for safety under Mr. Tubbs' car, Mrs. Flight stood guard over her petunia bed, and creaky Mr. McCavie dragged his garbage bags in from the curb. By the time they returned home, Jeremy was a dripping ball of sweat, and Cuddles was ready for a nice refreshing slurp from that magical bowl in the bathroom.

At suppertime, Cuddles planted himself next to the table as the family enjoyed the evening meal. He held one front paw gingerly in the air.

"I think that Cuddles might be sick," Jeremy said, clearly worried. "He hasn't touched one chunk of his special food, and Mr. Barkley said it was his favorite."

"A sick dog wouldn't beg," his mother said.

"That's right," his father agreed. "An ailing dog wouldn't sit there with a 'toss-me-a-measly-tidbit' look on his face. The brute is just testing the waters. Wants to see how much he can get away with. Ignore him."

Jeremy looked down at one lopsided ear that might or might not have toppled over from hunger. "I think he's telling us he wants human food," he said glumly. "Maybe he smells the peas."

His mother twisted the cap on the steak sauce. "Dogs don't usually beg for peas," she said. "I have a suspicion that Cuddles is hoping for something tastier." She held out a teeny sliver of meat gristle and the big dog gulped it down like he was famished.

"Here, boy." Jeremy offered a heftier slab, and again it disappeared down the gullet in one quick swallow. "Awesome! Look! He doesn't even chew! Come on, Dad, pony some up. You can see how much he loves it."

Mr. Jeffers pulled his plate in closer and circled it with his arms. "For one thing," he said firmly, "this steak is darn expensive. And for another thing, I didn't slave over a hot barbecue just to watch some finicky dog wolf down my prime rib. He'll eat his own food when he's good and hungry."

Jeremy tried to make Cuddles' lopsided ear stand up straight. "Ah, Dad, you're no fun! How would *you* like to choke down dried-up, tasteless old nuggets every single day of your life?"

"That's it! I can't stand those baleful eyes one second longer! Jeremy, fetch me a clean plate." Mrs. Jeffers grabbed her fork and went to work, stabbing morsels from around the table. Cuddles' lopsided ear zoomed right to the ceiling.

"Do you want your meat cut up in little chunks or big chunks, and how about a nice dab of peas? No, no, I'm not forgetting the mashed potatoes. Why don't I add a yummy dollop of butter to that? Now, don't gobble it up too fast. Save room for the pumpkin pie."

Mr. Jeffers watched in horror as his wonderful meal disappeared in dribs and drabs. When Jeremy snatched the juicy steak bone out from under his nose, that was the last straw.

"If Mr. Barkley doesn't show up bright and early on Monday mornig," he roared, "I will personally escort that dog home myself."

Not Your Everyday Ordinary Pet-Sitting Job

Freckles Flannigan stuck his head in the doorway, a big burlap bag in one hand and a cardboard box tucked under the other arm. Both appeared to be wiggling.

"We're going to visit my grandma for the weekend and she says Boo-Boo's not welcome," Freckles said, choking back tears. "Could he stay with you? My mom says she'll pay."

"Who's Boo-Boo?" Jeremy thought he heard scampering sounds coming from the box.

"Take him." Freckles handed Jeremy the bulging bag. "He's my sister's snake, but don't open it till you're inside."

"Where am I going to keep a snake?"

"The bathtub will do, only be sure to keep the shower curtain closed. Not everyone likes to see the fangs."

"Uh...what do I feed him?" Jeremy tried to ignore the queasy lump growing in his stomach.

"In the box," said Freckles. "Two mice a day should keep him happy. One if it's fat."

"Freckles, I...I don't know if this is a good idea." Jeremy felt the bag lurch and twitch in his hands. A snake with fangs wasn't exactly what he had in mind when he was thinking soft and cuddly. Just staring at the bag made him giddy. "Maybe I should check with my mom first," he said. "I mean, this isn't your everyday ordinary pet-sitting job."

Too late. When he looked up, Freckles was nowhere to be seen, and Jeremy was left with the uneasy feeling that he was clutching a whole wad of trouble. He held the bag as far away from his body as he could and headed straight for the phone.

Finally, after fourteen rings, an answer. "Hello."

"Murph, you gotta get over here on the double!"

"Can't. I'm in the middle of something important."

"My important is more important than your important!"

Murphy snickered. "I'm reading my sister's diary," he said. "Top that!"

"Yeah, well, I've got a wild snake trapped in a bag, and it's ready to chew my leg off!"

"Be over in two seconds!"

One look at the twisting burlap was enough to make Murphy wish he had never answered the dumb phone. "That thing is gonna burst out any minute," he said nervously. "You got a cage or tank or anything?"

Jeremy shook his head. "Freckles suggested the bathtub," he said. "There's one in the basement that no one ever uses, but we gotta hurry. Mom's next door, and she could be home any minute. Something tells me she might not be a big Boo-Boo fan."

Jeremy lugged the bag down the stairs, trying his best not to bounce it off the steps. Murphy followed with the wiggling box.

Jeremy set the bag in the tub and stepped back. "The main thing is to make sure Boo-Boo doesn't escape," he said. "Freckles said something about keeping the shower curtain closed, but that seems kind of chancy to me."

"Use duct tape," said Murphy. "My dad says it's strong enough to hold a house together. If we tape the shower curtain to the wall and the edge of the tub, there's no way that snake will ever escape."

Duct tape? Wow! Jeremy was impressed. Murph was turning into a regular Einstein.

It took the entire roll of sticky, gray tape before they were satisfied that the bathtub was one hundred percent escape-proof, but then an interesting dilemma arose.

"We've got a problem," Jeremy said. "For starters, Boo-Boo is still trapped inside the bag. And for another thing, how are we gonna feed him if we can't pull back the curtain?"

Murphy chewed his lip. This called for

super-serious thinking. "Have you actually *seen* this snake?" he asked.

"Well...no, but I know it's squirmy as heck."

"There you go," said Murphy. "It'll wiggle and worm its way right out of the bag, and besides, if Freckles tied that knot himself, Boo-Boo is probably already out playing in the tub by now."

Jeremy wasn't about to argue. The last thing he wanted to do was strip off six miles of tape and fiddle with that bag!

"And when it comes to food," Murphy said, lifting the lid from the box, "we can toss these up over the curtain rod. He'll think it's raining mice."

"No way!" Jeremy grabbed the box, and twelve pairs of beady red eyes stared up at him. "Look at them! They could be Frisket's brothers and sisters!"

"Don't be silly. These are mice. They've got tails. All that hamster had was a stub."

"Doesn't matter. I can't do it."

"You're making zero sense," said Murphy. "Freckles won't be back until Monday, and Boo-Boo's stomach will probably be rumbling by then. If he's this twitchy when he's happy, what do you think he'll be like when he's starving?"

Jeremy didn't care. He raced upstairs and returned a minute later with a box of Cheerios. He tossed a handful over the curtain rod and flicked a few in the box.

Surely Freckles would understand.

First thing the next morning, Jeremy crept down to the basement to check on things. When he peeked into the bathroom, sweat beads the size of raisins popped out all over his head.

The duct tape was still stuck tight to the wall, but down in the left-hand corner the plastic shower curtain was ripped to shreds. Jeremy stuck his head through the gaping hole. There on the bottom of the tub was the crumpled burlap bag and a smattering of Cheerios—but not a trace of the snake! Boo-Boo had made a clean getaway!

Jeremy bolted up over the stairs and collided headfirst with his mother in the hallway.

"Oh, there you are," Mrs. Jeffers said,

catching her breath. "I just had the most peculiar call from Mr. Tubbs. He phoned to say that poor Duffer has been missing since last night. He thought she might have wandered over here since she was so smitten with you."

Not Duffer! This whole day was turning into a nightmare! "Mom," he gasped, "could a snake swallow a cat?"

His mother raised an eyebrow. "What an odd question," she said. "Let's see...would that be a tiny kitten or a regular adult cat?"

"A humongous one," said Jeremy. "Like, oh, you know, like Duffer."

His mother laughed. "Perhaps you're reading too many wild adventure stories," she said. "Now off you go. I think I spotted Murphy lurking out on the front lawn."

Murphy looked like he had important stuff on his mind. "My baseball glove disappeared last night," he said, getting right down to business. "I usually poke it behind the rose bush, so I'm pretty sure it wasn't stolen."

"That's nothing! Boo-Boo escaped, and now Duffer is missing." Jeremy slumped down on the front steps. "Do you think any of this is related?"

"I think it's all your fault for not feeding him those mice," Murphy grumbled. "I told you Cheerios don't make good snake food. A hungry snake will probably pounce on anything!"

Jeremy buried his face in his hands. "I can't take all this responsibility," he moaned. "All I wanted was something soft and cuddly."

"It'll be different when you get your own pet," Murphy said. "Way different."

"Snakes are silly pets anyway," said Jeremy. "I was hiding it from Mom and Dad cause I thought they wouldn't want it in the house. Jeepers, I never actually saw it outside the bag. And besides, just being close to it made my heart pound so loud I couldn't even hear. What do you think Freckles' sister sees in that thing anyway?"

"I think it's time you told your parents," said Murphy. "You got yourself in way over your head on this one."

Jeremy blinked back tears. "Mom and Dad won't be too happy about the ripped shower curtain," he sputtered. "And now they'll probably tell me I have to wait till I'm older. I just know there's a pet out there for me somewhere, and I don't want some nutty old snake ruining my chances."

"Tell them anyway," Murphy said. "Otherwise, that mangy old Cuddles could be Boo-Boo's next meal."

They both giggled, although Jeremy's giggle was mixed with sniffles.

Jeremy shuffled his feet, blurted out the whole story in one long breath, and then waited for the bomb to drop.

Not a sound.

His mother looked like she had just bitten into a sour candy. His father looked like he really had to pee. And then their eyes met and they burst into laughter.

"So, does this mean you're not mad about the shower curtain?"

They shook their heads.

"And does this mean I haven't lost my chances of getting a real live pet of my own?"

They shook their heads again.

Jeremy was slightly confused. "Well, what *does* it mean?" he asked.

Mr. Jeffers tousled Jeremy's hair. "It means," he said, "that this is a prime example why you children don't come with instruction manuals. Why, no one could ever lift a book that fat, let alone fit it in the car to bring it home!"

Jeremy was as confused as ever. "But what about Duffer being eaten by Boo-Boo?"

"Oh, I take it you haven't heard the good news!" his mother said. "Mr. Tubbs found the cat in the back of a closet. She had kittens last night. Six roly-poly little tangerine tabbies, according to Mr. Tubbs."

"What about Murphy's baseball glove?" Jeremy asked. "That's still missing."

His father chuckled. "What young Murphy does with his belongings is a mystery to half the neighborhood. Every week it's something else!"

"Well...ah...uh...what about Boo-Boo? He's still on the missing list, and Freckles will be pretty upset."

"Boo-Boo can't have gone far," said his

mother. "We'll conduct a top to bottom search. Start with the laundry basket in the basement and work our way up to the attic. Dig through the boxes of Christmas decorations if we have to. It'll be like a big Easter egg hunt. And when we find him, your father will rig up a safe area out in the garage."

Jeremy didn't know what to say, what to think. All he knew was that the goose bumpy feeling he had been living with for the past two days was starting to disappear.

"Don't you worry, son," his father said. "Your only problem is your heart is too big." And that's not a bad thing at all.

The One

When two weeks passed without a neighbor appearing on the doorstep, Jeremy's feet started to drag. His mother became concerned when he walked by a fresh chocolate cake without even dabbing his finger in the icing. This moping had gone on long enough!

"Why don't you write a letter to your uncle Ray?" she suggested. "Maybe he has an animal on his farm who'd like to be adopted. People are always dropping off strays near his property."

Jeremy's father nearly choked on his coffee. "Hang on one dang minute!" he said, wiping coffee spittle from his chin. "Helen, you know your brother's a bit of a practical joker. Can we really trust him with something as important as this? Maybe you forgot, but the last time we asked for fresh eggs, he left a chicken on our lawn!"

"Nonsense!" Jeremy's mother had made up her mind. "I know my own brother and he wouldn't pull one of his foolish pranks where his favorite nephew is concerned. Write him a letter, Jeremy. Ray's coming to town next weekend anyway, so this is perfect timing."

That night Jeremy crawled into bed and began the most important letter of his life.

Dear Uncle Ray,

I was wondering if you had a spare pet on the farm who wouldn't mind moving to the city. I've crossed all these off my list so far:

Bird - Mom and Dad get too pushy and take it over. Actually, they go nuts.

Cat - But only because the hair makes me sneeze.

Guinea pig - They eat everything I own, and I mean everything!

Fish – Way too finicky and way too many instructions.

Hamster – Be okay if I could stay up all night and sleep all day!

Dog – Mom and Dad can't take one more slubby drool. I can't either!

Snake with fangs – You wouldn't believe that story if I told you!

Just so you know, what I'm really looking for is something soft and cuddly to snuggle up with in bed and read adventure stories to.

I'm counting on you, Uncle Ray. Mom says you're the animal expert! I'll love whatever you bring—promise!

See you soon,
Jeremy

All week long Jeremy felt like he was trapped in a bubble, floating along in slow motion. He fiddled with the hands on his watch, hoping to speed up time, but the minutes still acted like hours. Crossing off days on the calendar with big red Xs was even worse. This waiting business was driving him bonkers!

To help pass the time, he went to the library and checked out every new adventure book on the shelf...plus a few joke books too, just in case. Then he cleaned his room from top to bottom, even laying an old blanket over his bed lest his mother complain about pet hairs. Everything had to be perfect!

This was different from looking after Mr. McCavie's guinea pig or Mr. Barkley's dog. This pet wasn't going home after two days. It was going to be all his, all the time. He would be known around the neighborhood as nine-year-old Jeremy Jeffers, responsible pet owner!

On Saturday morning, Uncle Ray's rickety farm truck sputtered up the driveway, blue smoke spewing out the rear. Jeremy craned his neck through his bedroom window, hoping to catch a glimpse of something soft and cuddly in the front seat.

Nothing.

Lickety split, fast as lightning, his feet

flew down over the stairs, nearly knocking his father over in his rush to squeeze past him in the doorway.

"Uncle Ray!" he yelled. "My pet! Did you bring my new pet?"

Uncle Ray winked and bent over to lift something from the floor of the cab. "Catch your breath," he said, opening the door and getting out. "You look like you're about to explode!" He carefully laid a small card-board box on the ground and slowly opened the flaps. "Now Jeremy, I'll warn you now, this may take some getting used to."

Jeremy swallowed hard. The butterflies in his stomach were as big as bats, and they were trying to flap up through his throat.

His mother broke the silence. "Merciful heavens, Ray," she gasped, glancing over his shoulder. "What is that? Some sort of giant rat you discovered out in the barn?" She fanned herself with the tail of her apron.

Uncle Ray lifted an odd gray creature out of the box and blew warm breath over its head. The thing licked his mustache and purred like a freight train. "It's a cat," he said proudly. "And a particularly handsome one at that."

Jeremy's father took a step backwards. "But it's…it's bare-naked! Stick it back in the box, Ray. It's giving me the willies!"

Uncle Ray tickled a pair of enormous, pointy ears. "Granted, it's not your everyday furry variety," he said, passing the muscular little animal to Jeremy. "It's a Sphynx, one of those hairless breeds. Got him from the vet who visits the farm. Said it might be the perfect thing for a boy with allergies."

Jeremy tentatively ran his hand over the warm, wrinkly skin. "Uh…Uncle Ray," he whispered, almost afraid to ask, "where's the soft and cuddly part?"

Uncle Ray grinned. "Hang on a second. You've got your Aunt Doris to thank in that department. She's been knitting up a storm all week."

He pulled out a shopping bag from behind the driver's seat. Jeremy peeked and saw fuzzy mounds of yellow, orange, red, purple and green. His uncle slipped a teensy mohair sweater over the cat's head and reached back into the bag.

"And look what she knit with all the left-over bits of wool!" he said, holding up a matching sweater. It was the perfect fluffy fit for a nine-year-old. The swirls of color reminded Jeremy of his favorite candy.

"Jellybeans!" Jeremy cried, blurting the first thing that popped into his mind. "His name will be Jellybean!"

The little cat purred and attached himself to Jeremy's neck. Jeremy snuggled back. This might not be a hefty fur ball like Duffer, but Jeremy knew in his heart that the perfect pet had just come into his life, and he wasn't going to waste one second. He marched into the house to introduce Jellybean to his new home.

That night, Jellybean lay purring on Jeremy's chest. The little cat opened one sleepy eye and thanked his lucky stars, for he had found the most perfect boy in the whole world: soft and cuddly, warm and fuzzy, and, best of all, this boy loved adventure stories too. Jellybean nuzzled closer and soon both boy and cat were fast asleep, snug inside their cozy mohair sweaters.

Dear Reader,

With the exception of the snake, all the animals in this book are based on those I have owned. I really did have a guinea pig who chewed all the knobs off the television remote and a chirpy blue budgie who perched on my husband's shoulder each evening while he did the daily crossword puzzle. But unlike Beauty-in-the-Book, my budgie *never* chirped the answers!

While I've never owned a moving mountain like Cuddles, I do have a ragamuffin pooch named Luke, who, like Cuddles, wolfed down a chocolate Easter bunny and then—surprise, surprise!—threw up the entire gooey mess on the carpet. But

Cuddles was actually lucky because chocolate can make dogs very sick. I had to bundle poor Luke up in a blanket and dash off to the animal hospital. In the end, that two-dollar chocolate bunny turned into an expensive vet bill. Now we are very careful about keeping all chocolate out of reach of sniffy wet noses.

Yes, pets are fun to own, but keeping them safe, healthy and happy doesn't happen by accident. It's important to learn all you can about your animal. You've probably noticed that Jeremy didn't always know a lot about the pet he was caring for.

For example, when Jeremy snatched a steak bone off his father's plate, Cuddles may have been in his glee (what dog doesn't love a fat chewy bone?), but this was actually a big fat no-no. Animal bones like steak bones can splinter and hurt a dog from the inside. Please forgive poor Jeremy. He didn't know this. If he had chosen a dog for a pet, I have a strong feeling that he would have gone to the library in search of a pet care book. Maybe one called, *How to Care for the Best Dang Dog in the Whole*

Wide World. Jeremy would have learned all about buying safe pet store bones, about how mashed potatoes and peas aren't the best food choices, and a whack of other useful tidbits.

Since this book was written, I have gotten a new puppy. Hugo is a Chihuahua, the smallest dog breed in the world, and even though he speeds through the house like a tornado, he also loves to snuggle. You know, the more I think about it, the more I think that Hugo would have been the perfect pet for Jeremy.

What about you? Do you think Jeremy would have changed his mind about dogs, guinea pigs, or whatever, if you showed up on his doorstep with your pet? Why not write me a letter, care of Orca Book Publishers (you'll find their address on the copyright page), telling exactly what makes your animal the number-one best pet ever! And while you're at it, Luke and Hugo would especially like to learn new hiding places for dirty socks.

Nancy Shouse wrote *Any Pet Will Do* as a tribute to her dying guinea pig, Rex, and to all the pets she's enjoyed over the years. The novel was written one magical summer while most of her family was away for ten weeks taking part in History Television's "Quest for the Sea," a reality show depicting life in an isolated fishing outport in 1937. Nancy lives in St. John's, Newfoundland, where, she says, "Rumor has it that some mighty creative juices blow in off the Atlantic Ocean mingled with the drizzle and fog."